Sponsors

Photographers
Ameerah Shabazz- Bilal
Barbara McClane
Nzima Hutchings

Nzima Hutchings
Visionary, Founder of
LAWR Magazine & Every Kinda Lady LLC

EVERY KINDA LADY LLC
FELLOWS & MEMBERS CARD
- INKWELL: ALL ACCESS WRITER
- WRITER'S TRIBE: WRITER'S CAFE (ONLY)
- OF BREATH AND PAGE: WRITE TO WELLNESS & WRITER'S CAFE
- RETREATER'S PEN: LITERARY ART WELLNESS RETREATS (ONLY)

+1 860-800-LADY

Literary Art Wellness Advocate & Educator
Virtual Creative Writing Room Café
Sage Circle Storytelling
Wellness Writing Coach Master Trainer
Expressionist Facilitator
RSS Poetry & Meditative Writing Groups
Transformative Women Writing Workshops
Somatic Writing & Body Vision Boards
Literary Art Retreat Coordinator
Customized Business Journals & Publishing
Developmental Editor
Line Editing (content, context flow)
Beta Reading Party Coordinator
Literary Production Management
Poet Laureate of Enfield CT. 2023-2025
Hartford Book Festival Visionary Organizer/Curator
Sexual Assault Counselor | HVN Facilitator | RSS | Alternative to Suicide Facilitator

Nzima Sherylle Hutchings

~Mission Statement~

Every Kinda Lady Literary Art Wellness Weekender Magazine: is dedicated to celebrating and amplifying women's voices through the transformative power of literary art. We advocate for the holistic well-being of women, emphasizing both individual and collective wellness and healing. Our magazine promotes mindfulness and evocative art that opens the mind, stimulates inner analysis, and fosters joy in writing as a means to wellness. We empower women to tell their stories and publish their perspectives, while providing a platform for literary and visual art submissions. Our aim is to build a literary legacy and blueprint for self-expression, creating a vibrant community committed to wellness, creativity, and empowerment.

Copyright©,2024 Nzima Hutching, Every Kinda Lady. All rights are reserved. No photocopying, scanning, or reproduction of materials.

Production Manager, Content &
Chief Editor
Nzima Hutchings
Every Kinda Lady LLC
N'zimah Sensory Essentials
Enfield, CT.

SELECT CONTENT PAGES

Cuba by Ameerah Shabazz-Bilal pg. 5

Cuba Art, Music, Culture pg. 10-16

Morning Pg. 17-20

Every Kinda Lady Writing Paths to Healing pg. 21-24

Ekphrastic Poetry Snap, Paste & Write: Poetic Optics by Master Teaching Artists" pg. 25-31

About Ameerah Shabazz-Bilal & When Women Speak pg. 32-33

Her Smokin Tongue in Spanish:(EKL & WWS members) pg. 34-55

When Women Speak / Every Kinda Lady Poetic Writing Prompt Pg. 56-58

Pedal On(Poem) Poet Laureate Nzima Hutchings Pg. 59

Every Kinda Lady: Anthropological Tongue: Vignettes with Voice Integrity Pg. 60-61

Assata Shakur Quotes to Prompt pages 62-64

Junk Journals, Creative Writing & Mindfulness pg. 65-67

Evocative Writing and Imagery pg. 68-70

Top View Writing Prompt Pg. 71

When Women Speak

When Women Speak Poetry Anthology
Volume 1

Authored and Edited by Ameerah Shabazz-Bilal

"Reach out to Ameerah Shabazz-Bilal to find out how you can participate in the When Women Speak Writer's Retreat, contribute to the poetry anthology, or join her poetic platforms."

Cuba

"Why you take my picture?", one asks. I say because you are Cuban. She says: "How do you know that because I stand here?" I say no, because everything in Cuba is beautiful as are you, so you MUST be Cuba! She smiles and says - go ahead - take my picture. Our hearts are pleased.

I snapped a shot with each inquisitive smile from the land of brown smiles and artful colors - that's photojournalism

Snap!

The fiber of Cuba, a mystery to me. I learned their blood runs rims of bipolarism - Cubans Love Fidel. Cubans also hate Fidel - it's ambivalence with reason. Folks gather in Revolution Square, as youths shout:

"Soy Fidel, Soy Revolución, Soy Cuba!"

To my American eye for once, there is no color—
only witnessing the unity, solidarity, and vibrant proclamation:

I Am Cuba!

As flailing multicolored arms, hearts, and souls rejoice—

Soy Cuba!

I feel Revolution may have tried, but it could not quiet racial identity—which breathes with an untethered spirit. When we Americans think of Cuba, we think - bright, scrappy, intense, and shrewd. But the breath of this island is the Malecon the spirit of the crumbling pastel and gray-colored buildings all around, "oh, the colors"! they pulse like bold strokes of art!

I understand how HE is hated and loved precisely because he was Cuban. Cubans don't have the same caste system as my American mind - you are either Cuban or you are not. But in that, colonization has left some mark on the Afro-Cuban - which gives him the right of passage with Cuban blood, ancestry, crumbled buildings, and hidden not-so-hidden places in a caste system which mimics some familiarity to my American eye - lighter is better….but the beautiful hues and eyes, and skin and hair of Afro'ism scream a wondrous beauty - it too matched the buildings - the art - the colors - the rhythms and sounds of hips that know how to shake and swirl.

One mouth utters, almost shouting - "BEFORE HIM - we 'the African' had nothing. He split that and gave to the people". Someone else yelled - "That was the beginning of the promise, that promise had murder in it too". But I, I remember Assata fleeing, I remember Malcolm's words and Frederick Douglas', too who urged Africans in America to go and fight for and with Cuba for independence and the end of oppression - I laugh inside because once again it's there - the mind chains of ourselves the darker brother in the Americas under oppression yet so oblivious that we would be urged to go fight for someone else's liberation and keep the chains ourselves.

But Cuba was to be the promised land for 'the African' in America - there's the connection. However, lynched that hope may have been - it cried into centuries of blood with edges of hate. Black people, don't necessarily hate the hate that hate made - they want to love freedom.

So they will love that HE the father of this small blackened nation made by white flight reached across ocean and fear to 'the continent'. Nelson Mandela was touched, 40,000 thousand sent by Castro is what is on the minds....Afro-Cubans love him. Ask them why not leave the island? - they will say "It's home". The ivory side fled the 90-mile distance to the shore of America and still cry and mourn as they will not return. We question, who is the murderer? Who is the wrongdoer, and who will or can set anybody free?

"Sin dejar de ser cubanos": Without ceasing to be Cuban
Garveyism is Cuba - for Cuba is raceless - Garveyism died in the lukewarm sea of the Malecon taking with it some of the spurs of liberty - but the trade was made.

People remember: Mandela said, "HE Cuba's father destroyed the myth of the invincibility of the white oppressor."

People forgot the smell of a cigar, not one could be found. But No one questioned the irony of no cigar but drugs on every corner, this is no coincidence.

But me, I look at the beautiful crumbling architecture, the art-painted buildings, and brown faces and hearts and I see the rainbows of people and the smiles and the children who are allowed to play at night.

I look at the secret homemade boats made to float which steal away into the night, and maybe 90 miles is not that far away.

I see stores with empty shelves,
Milk and liquor are what they sell.
The milk feeds the babies,
The liquor feeds the soul of the parents who have only what they grow and hustle for to eat - I wonder who told this lie.

Men in white, with multicolored beads swinging from their necks—
Babalawo, Yoruba priests called upon by abuelas, heal with sacred rites…
diaspora beauty, holistic connections—
chicken eggs, rum-sprayed breaths offered in Hammel Alley's corners.

Cuban drumbeats pulse through Elegguá, through Orisha shrines, and the island's single small mosque—

they form the spine of Cuba, the heartbeat of its spirit.

I listen for the smile hidden in the rhythm of those drums. I think sugar in the blood has a different meaning in the smile of a brown face,
for the tongue remembers how it earned its color from blood and fight.
Cuban smiles waver between *"the promise'* and the prayer of *Patria y Vida!*

The Cuban smile is resilient, caught between hope and survival.

Children play, sweeping the streets with laughter—
they are the living art of human existence, born from
the crumbles of decay and gleaming curves of convertibles along the seawall. Their laughter stirs up waves; their tears fill the Malecon Sea.

My camera lens overflows with you!

I hear music on every corner and smiles and laughter way into the night. Where hips sway and children play and families convene - I wonder, is this happiness? I know this is Cuba!

The revolution is in music, let it praise revolution. But Be ready, they are blood songs. Song melodies of Aretha in the key of Ceclia the darker sister the Queen not from Spanish Harlem but from the belly and guts of Havana...she sang freedom songs,

Cecilia Cruz, Cecilia Cruz -
did they hear you? Songs of - lady liberty!

"The revolution has returned"! - someone yells - "this is a protest!

Communism MUST go"! Only to be followed by firecracker sounds and silence before wails - and I wonder, am I on the street in America, or has the revolution finally been televised?

I'm reminded not to take sides - it's foolish as I'm traumatized from my own oppression which some want to pretend doesn't exist.   So I resist the urge to yell:

Freedom, freedom, freedom - Libertad, Libertad, Libertad!
And I remember both are the language of the colonizer.

And I remember the question - "why do you take our pictures",
And I remember the response too: "Because Cuba is beautiful".

Beautiful Santerías, draped in purity, glide in white along the streets—
her presence weaving through lives patterned across the Malecon.
Oh, how the white of the robes swell like mist over the sea,
then rises like clouds, returning with ancestral spirit in each breath of Cuban color.

And oh, the colors! They pulse like bold strokes of art!
Revolution may try, but it cannot quiet racial identity—
  -   it breathes in untethered spirit.

Here I stand, Black in Cuba—
There you stand, Black in Cuba—
our smiles resonate with the familiarity of kindred souls.

I know you are Cuban from the reflection of your soul.

Tú eres Cuba. Tú soy de Cuba.
Cuba is beautiful as are you, so you MUST be Cuba!
   -   SNAP - !

©2022 Ameerah Shabazz-Bilal

DON PEPE'S TOBACCO FARM

PAPITA'S COFFEE FARM

When Women Speak

Retreat 2023 Sisterhood Horsing Around, Self-care, Fresh Cigars & Farm to Table Food

PAGE 10

When
W♡MEN
Speak

RETREAT BEACH RELAX

RETREAT MALECON

CUBAN HOSPITALITY WITH LOCALS AND DAYRON ROBLES OWNER OF THE AIRBNB

Retreat 2023

Cuba Olympic Track winner

EAT LAUGH

When
W♡MEN
Speak

RETREAT WRITE RELAX

PAGE 11

Art & Music

When Women Speak Poetry Performance
Sculptor/Artist: Lee & Yary Cantautora Studio Ameerah Shabazz-Bilal
Havana, Cuba

Enfield, CT. Poet Laureate Nzima Hutchings, in Havana, Cuba, July 16th, 2023. Photo by Helena Lewis.
Sculptor/Artist: Lee Cantautora

Yary MCCARTHY

Yaramis Velázquez McCarthy, known as Yary McCarthy, is a Cuban songwriter from Cienfuegos, now based in Havana. She performs at various venues while building a dedicated following for her music. Alongside her husband, acclaimed visual artist Leonardo G. Márquez (Leo Escultor), she runs an art gallery at Neptuno 511, Central Havana. Every Friday, they host "Peña Semilla Nueva," celebrating diverse artists from Cuba and beyond, including recent guest Chinoy from Chile. Yary is currently writing new songs for her upcoming CD, bringing her next dream closer to reality.

MARIA ESTRELLA - ARTIST (LADY W/FLOWERS IN HER HAIR)
Visiting Cuba is a dream realized. It's been on my bucket list for years, and now being here with a group of talented artists for the Havana Biennial is an honor. As someone with Cape Verdean roots, I'm thrilled to explore Cuba's vibrant arts, music, and culinary heritage, reflecting deep cultural connections. The first time I visited Cape Verde it showed our connection with Cuba through Education and the Arts. I am super excited to be here.

PAGE 13

CULTURE

AFRO CUBAN

When Women Speak

BEYOND ROOTS

BUSINESS IS LOCATED IN LAMPARILLA 404 BETWEEN BERNAZA AND VILLEGAS, OLD HAVANA

ADRIANA HEREDIA SÁNCHEZ
JOSÉ LUIS CORREDERA

MERCHANDISE | SERVICES | SPIRITUAL & CULTURAL TOURS
CLOTHES, ART, GIFTWARE, AND HAIR CARE

Drums photo: Every Kinda Lady Nzima

PAGE 14

Photo by: Ameerah Shabazz-Bilal

Santeria, an Afro-Cuban Religion

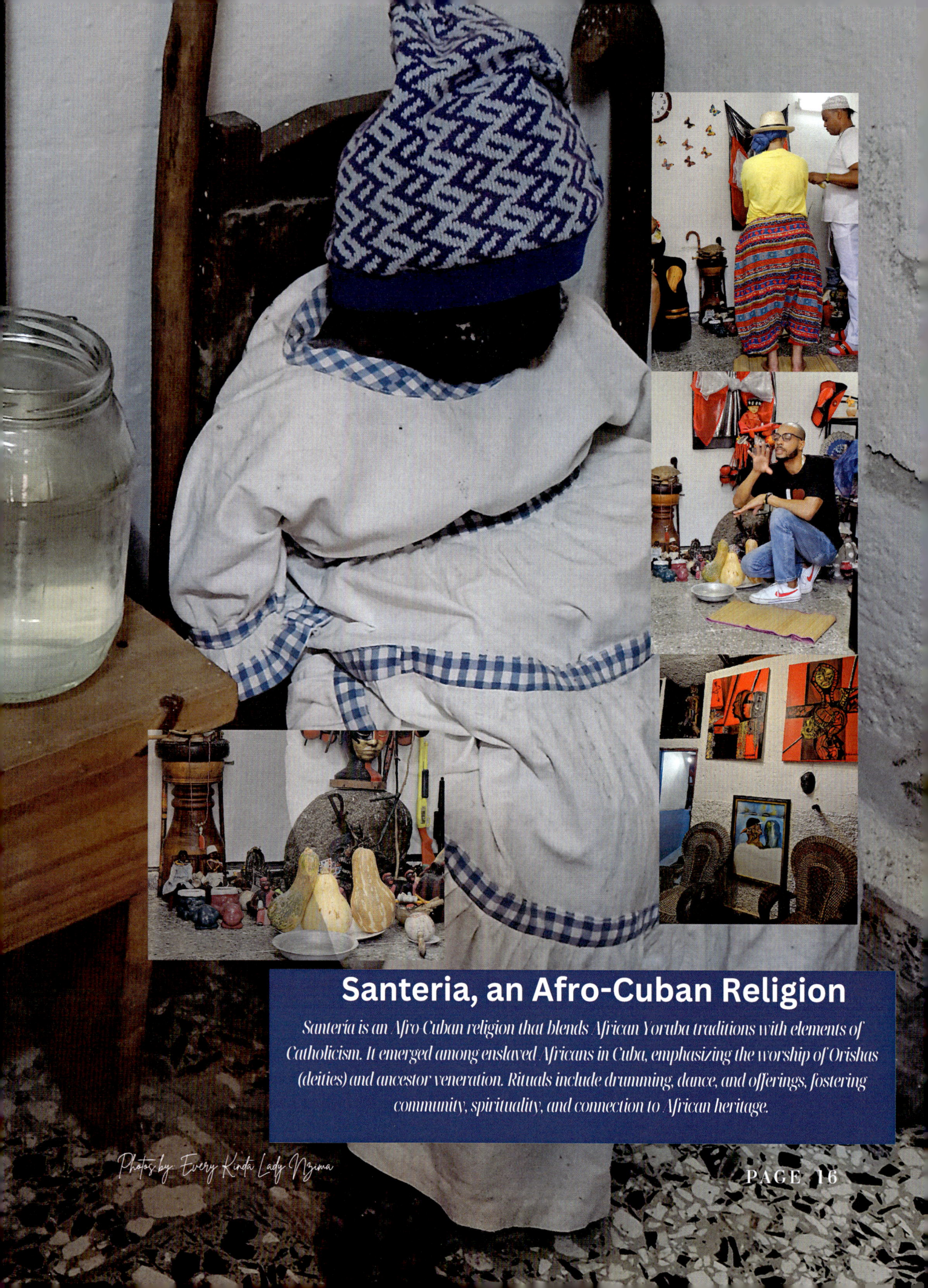

Santería is an Afro-Cuban religion that blends African Yoruba traditions with elements of Catholicism. It emerged among enslaved Africans in Cuba, emphasizing the worship of Orishas (deities) and ancestor veneration. Rituals include drumming, dance, and offerings, fostering community, spirituality, and connection to African heritage.

Photos by Every Kinda Lady Nzima

PAGE 16

MORNING PAGES

DAWNING RESILIENCE & WAVES
BY NZIMA HUTCHINGS

In the quiet dawn, where the aroma of Cuban coffee mingles and matches the richness of her skin, a young woman sits with her dainty wrist cradling a pen. She is a tapestry of resilience, her spirit woven from the whispers of ancestors. Morning pages unfurl like waves, carrying the weight of oceanic thoughts—each word a drop of saltwater, each sentence a pearl unearthed from the sea bed of her soul.

Her hands, small yet mighty, navigate the depths of her inner landscape, where wounds echo like distant thunder. Here, in this sacred space, she finds the courage to voice her truth, to speak to the water goddess, the deity who cradles her dreams and sorrows alike. Clutched within her, the unyielding strength of generations pulses—an unbroken lineage of resilient women who have danced through storms and basked in sunlight.

Unsalted and unbothered, she remains untethered to the world's noise, anchored instead by the roots of her heritage. The sunflowers sway outside, nodding in rhythm with her thoughts, their golden faces a reflection of her inner light. As she writes her way out of the depths, the ocean becomes her confidant, each wave a reminder that she, too, is vast and enduring, capable of shaping the shores of her destiny.

In this communion of ink and water, she conjures magical tales—stories of survival, of joy, of the delicate balance between the weight of the past and the promise of tomorrow. With each stroke of her pen, she weaves a narrative that honors her lineage, embraces her complexities, and ultimately, celebrates the beauty of being unshackled and free.

Morning Pages w/ Deep Breathing

Pour out your secrets on the pages—let it flow where you feel both safe and brave. Begin the healing. Craft stories, weave poetry, and sketch vignettes; let your razor-sharp tongue spill the ink of your truth like crimson from a blade, and then butterfly forward into the light.

Keep or toss pages away...

Instructions

1. **Find Your Space:** Choose a quiet spot with a warm drink—coffee, tea, or lemonade.

2. **Grab Your Tools:** Use a journal or loose paper and a flowing pen. This is not the time for typing.

3. **Deep Breathing Exercise (1 Minute):**
Sit comfortably, feet flat, hands in your lap.
Close your eyes or lower your gaze.
Inhale deeply through your nose for a count of four. Hold for four.
Exhale slowly through your mouth for sx.
Repeat three times, releasing tension with each exhale.

4. **Set Your Intention:** Breathe deeply again, knowing this is a space for release and transformation.

5. **Write Freely:** Begin writing without hesitation. Don't worry about edits, sharing, or grammar. Let your thoughts flow—dreams, worries, ideas.

6. **Embrace the Rabbit Hole:** Follow any tangents or associations. This is your space to explore.

7. **Let Go:** Release worries onto the page, imagining them floating away.

8. **Stay Present:** Focus on the act of writing, grounding yourself in the moment.

9. **End with Gratitude:** Reflect on what you've written and express gratitude for this time.

10. **Routine is Key:** Aim to make this a daily practice to start your day centered.

Remember, this is a personal journey—write boldly and allow your mind to transform with every stroke of the pen.

PAGE 18

LAWR Morning Journal

IMMERSE YOURSELF IN THE PRACTICE OF A FOCUSED MORNING JOURNAL—A POWERFUL TOOL THAT CAN POSITIVELY SHAPE YOUR MINDSET AND WELL-BEING.

(Day): _____ (Month): _____ (Year): _____

Today's Affirmation

Goal of the day

(To Do) Priority of the day:

_____

_____

_____

(Thoughts)
SET INTENTIONS FOR CLARITY, VITALITY, AND INNER PEACE, AND FEEL THE POSITIVE IMPACT THROUGHOUT THE DAY.

(Morning Rituals Checklist)
ROADMAP TO AN ENERGIZED AND PURPOSEFUL START.

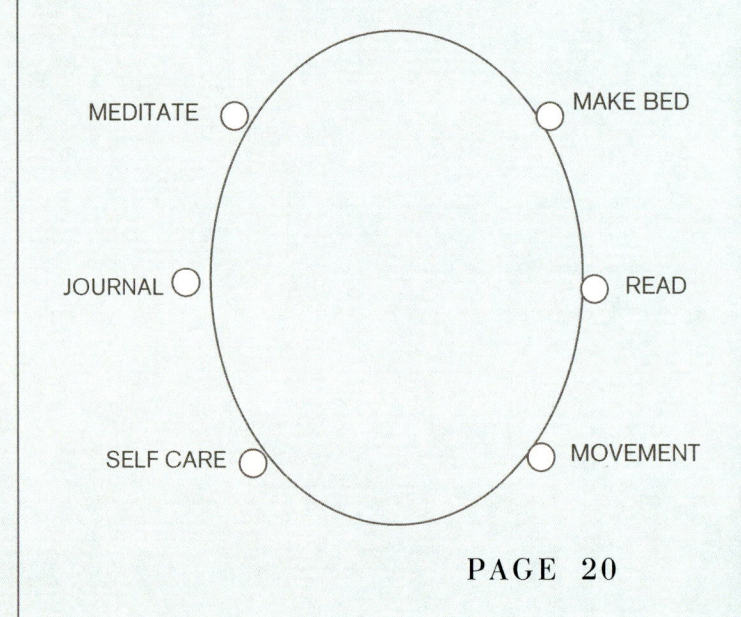

- MEDITATE
- MAKE BED
- JOURNAL
- READ
- SELF CARE
- MOVEMENT

PAGE 20

Nzima's Path to Poetry, Resiliency Writing and Self-care

I started writing poetry to write out my lived experiences.

I began my journey as a writer from a place of deep pain—a pain I could no longer hold in the fibers of my being. It was spine-tingling and soul-bending. At first, my writing was intensely personal, a way to release the turmoil I felt inside. As a poet, I played with language, crafting words that felt almost encrypted, holding my secrets close while whispering them into the world.

Over time, I discovered that writing was not just a means of expression but a powerful healing tool.

In those quiet moments of reflection, I found strength and a sense of control I had longed for. I realized that sitting in the hiding corners of shame, guilt, and ego was far more painful than the act of telling my story. Each word I wrote gave me permission to own my truths—my truths, my family's truths, and the essence of my authentic self.

Writing became my pathway to active acceptance. I wanted to live—not just exist but truly embrace life in all its complexities.

Many women are drawn to share their own stories. Many needing moments to release, memories that linger in the heart. If I could offer one piece of advice, it would be this: "Write without fear."

Nzima's path to poetry & resiliency writing continues.

Put pen to paper and let your emotions flow freely. Don't worry about editing or how others might perceive you. Don't let the fear of hurting someone or getting it all right hold you back. This is your journey of creative release, self-expression, and, ultimately, freedom.

The process of writing can be daunting. You may face doubts and insecurities, but remember that vulnerability breeds strength. It's okay to stumble; it's okay to be messy. What matters is that you start. When you give yourself the permission to express your truth, you not only heal yourself but also create a ripple effect, inspiring others to do the same.

In this shared act of storytelling, we connect with one another. We realize that our experiences, while unique, resonate deeply with others. Every story matters, and your voice is vital in this collective narrative of humanity.
So, I encourage all: embrace your pain, celebrate your victories, and write your truth. You never know how your words might resonate with someone else, lighting the way for their own journey toward healing and acceptance.

Pam Aisha Hudson: Path to Writing and Self-care

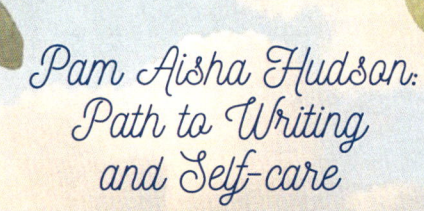

Writing has always been a path for healing and growth. God willing, I'll soon be traveling to Cuba for a writer's retreat, where I look forward to immersing myself in the vibrant culture and history of the island. Retreats are rejuvenating experiences for me, providing space to reflect deeply and focus on personal growth. With the rich backdrop of Cuba, I anticipate inspiration at every turn. I'm eager to meet new people, reconnect with familiar faces, and explore opportunities for meaningful connections in what promises to be a socially enriching and creatively stimulating experience.

Barbara McClane
Path to Self-Care

I have found Cuba to be one of the most vibrant places a photographer could visit. The cultural structure is rich in bold colors that pop, making the streets feel like a canvas, full of artistry. As a photographer, I became passionate about capturing the beauty and seizing captivating scenes as they unfolded. Between clicks of the camera, I reflected on how photography and wellness resonate within my spirit, focusing on mindfulness, creativity, and the spiritual connection needed to capture the perfect image.

Spanish Version

He descubierto que Cuba es uno de los lugares más vibrantes que un fotógrafo puede visitar. Su estructura cultural está llena de colores audaces que resaltan, haciendo que las calles se vean como un lienzo, lleno de arte. Como fotógrafa, me apasiona capturar la belleza y escenas cautivadoras mientras suceden. Entre los clics de la cámara, reflexiono sobre cómo la fotografía y el bienestar se entrelazan en mi espíritu, prestando atención a la atención plena, la creatividad y la conexión espiritual necesaria para capturar la imagen perfecta.

Ekphrastic poetry is a form of poetry that responds to or describes a work of art, such as a painting, sculpture, or photograph. The term "ekphrasis" comes from the Greek word for "description," and these poems often aim to convey the emotional impact of the artwork, interpret its meaning, or explore the relationship between the visual and literary forms.

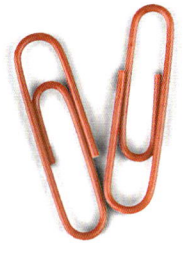

Snap Paste Write

Instructions
- Take a Photo: Capture an image of something eye-catching or artful that inspires you—a vibrant mural, a serene landscape, or a unique object.
- Write About It: Reflect on the photo you've taken. Consider the emotions it evokes, the story behind it, or the memories it brings to mind.

*Snap
Paste
Write*

*UNLEASH YOUR VISUAL ART!
LET IT COME ALIVE, POSING
AND DANCING AS YOUR MUSE,
INSPIRING EVERY WORD OF
YOUR LITERARY CREATIONS!*

EKPHRATIC POETRY
RAZORBLADE BUTTERFLY LADY

Does the span of my wings cut you,
rebanar you,
as I fly beyond stars,
outside the low and grow?
You see me being the best me
living and surviving through adversity
yet, you make it about you, always a wild sideshow
tweak roles and truths
At times your eyes
reveal designs of defeat, when there's no need
there's no deny you silently compete
Thought together we'd be
two negro butterflies flying high
yet, you set yourself on fire
maintain being a master storyteller, a liar
talking out your throat
it seems I motivate your bold,
you play the extreme wanting to be seen,
selling your soul,
moving on ego—
esparcir,
spread and abrir,
open to close green-eyed vibes,
to silence low-flying frequencies.
the hating and childlike sneaky tendencies
Divorce the metamorphosis to be me
My razor blade sharp 3rd eye see you,
and sadly, I loved you.... still do
we went through cocooning and buffooning together
weathered storms while sticking out our chest
I gave space and open access,
all the while in my space you played my face
you are clever, a natural talent
yet I won't overlook your antics,
the way you twist words
into a pretzel of confusion,
taking it too far—
have me wanting to cortar,
give you walking papers,
and say bye, boo.

Enfield, CT. Poet Laureate
Nzima Hutchings

Ekphrastic Poetry Photo Prompts

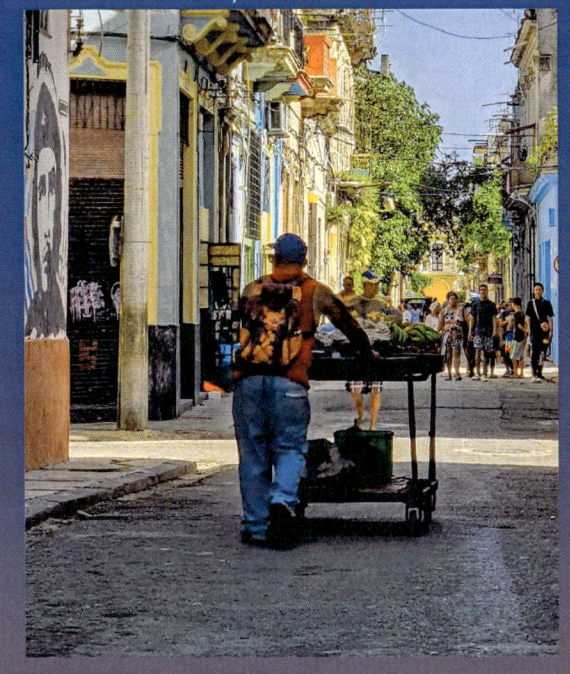

Poetic Optics
MUSE
Barkel McClane
PHOTOGRAPHY

PAGE 29

Ekphrastic Poetry Photo Prompts

Poetic Optics
MUSE
Ameerah Shabazz-Bilal

When ♥
W♥MEN
Speak

PAGE 30

Ekphrastic Poetry Photo Prompts

Poetic Optics
MUSE

PAGE 31

When Women Speak
Ameerah Shabazz-Bilal

Ameerah Shabazz-Bilal is an award-winning poet, visual artist, and educator from Newark, NJ. She is the recipient of EvoluCulture's 2024 Women in Poetry Award, the 2024 Hartford Literary Service Award, and the Maria Mazziotti Gillan Literary Service Award. Her poetry has been featured at major festivals, including The Dodge Poetry Festival, North 2 Shore, and Yale University Poetry/Slam Festivals. Internationally, she has performed in Cuba at El Jelengue Hall of the Patio Areito EGREM. As the founder of "When Women Speak" and "When People Speak," Ameerah has created platforms for diverse voices. She is also the author of *Breathing Through Concrete* and *When Women Speak Anthology*. Her work has been published in *NY Writers Coalition*, *Soul Spaces*, *Every Kinda Lady*, and more. Ameerah is an NJPAC Teaching Artist and will be featured in upcoming events such as the 2024 Dodge Poetry Festival, Lagos International Poetry Festival, Havana Biennial Art Festival, Newark Arts Festival, and Paterson Poetry continuing to elevate poetry and cultural narratives worldwide. narratives worldwide.

Spanish Translation

Ameerah Shabazz-Bilal es una poeta, artista visual y educadora galardonada de Newark, NJ. Es receptora del Premio Mujeres en Poesía de EvoluCulture 2024, el Premio al Servicio Literario de Hartford 2024 y el Premio al Servicio Literario Maria Mazziotti Gillan. Su poesía ha sido presentada en festivales importantes, incluidos el Dodge Poetry Festival, North 2 Shore y los Festivales de Poesía/Slam de la Universidad de Yale. Internacionalmente, ha actuado en Cuba en El Jelengue Hall del Patio Areito EGREM. Como fundadora de "When Women Speak" y "When People Speak", Ameerah ha creado plataformas para voces diversas. También es autora de *Breathing Through Concrete* y *When Women Speak Anthology*. Su trabajo ha sido publicado en *NY Writers Coalition*, *Soul Spaces*, *Every Kinda Lady* y más. Ameerah es una Teaching Artist de NJPAC y estará presente en eventos como el Dodge Poetry Festival 2024, el Lagos International Poetry Festival, el Havana Biennial Art Festival, el Newark Arts Festival y el Paterson Poetry, continuando así la elevación de la poesía y las narrativas culturales a nivel mundial.

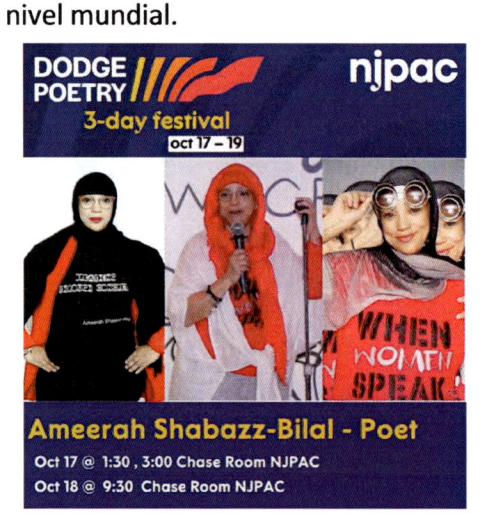

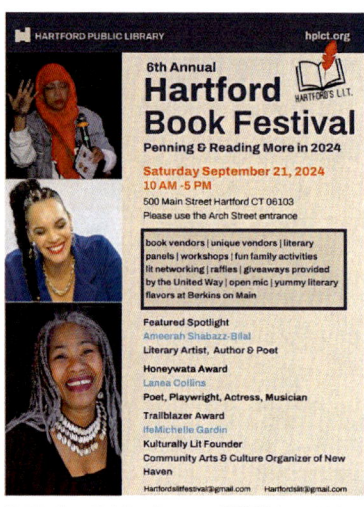

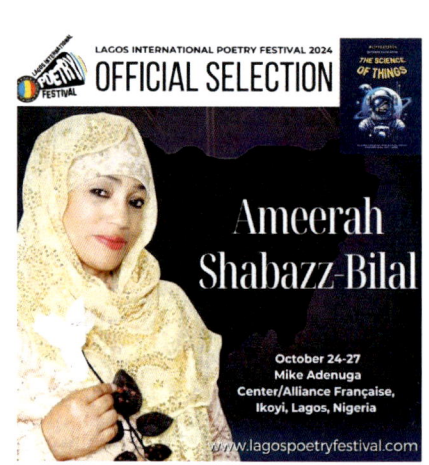

When Women Speak

So, What's It All About?

When Women Speak, is a platform for women from ALL backgrounds and experiences. It provides the stage for female poets, artists and creatives. Voices are heard, sometimes found, but ALWAYS encouraged to SPEAK their truths. WHEN WOMEN SPEAK hosts a variety of women with diverse voices - unapologetically. We are here to create an empowerment movement, offering safe spaces for women to grow themselves, share, and empower others. We as women know, empowering women offers the change the world needs. We are a primal force - When Women Speak.

Poetry

HER SMOKIN' TONGUE IN SPANISH

Without Accent

The children danced amongst the thick, rolling accents
wrapped around their ears like a lullaby of tongues,
never realizing they were bilingual,
as the voices slipped away,
blending into the wind and scattering out into the world—
vanishing once they stepped off *The Block*,
out from the nest that held them.

They were dropped there, planted like seeds—
into the soil of accents and syllables,
into the gracious arms and warm hugs of the hermanas. .
There was one who carried a barren field,
a womb that wept in dry seasons,
nourished by tears from seven streams
that flowed freely frequently in pain.
Dehydrated and replenished with words and dreams,
and prayers,
and hugs,
and more prayers.

Yet they never softened the arid plains of her garden.
But there was arroz con frijoles
and leche evaporada mixed with water,
"sweet milk" on children's tongues—
already stained with Farina mustaches and plátano kisses.

PAGE 35

The kids bundled together like bowls of raisins—
dark, sweet, and nearly indistinguishable,
except for one.
No one knew his origins,
but he stayed—his roots planted in their dirt,
bright face glowing like sunshine drippings.
They gave him their name,
the only thing that was theirs to give.

In that crowded corner, they molded themselves into family,
shaped from bits of laughter and struggle—
from Johnny Cake, buñuelos, and whispers of shared bread.
He swallowed their stories, tasted the crumbs of their lives,
until his skin, his smile, his very being looked just like them—
And the womb, once dry, smiled and fell silent,
no more tears,
only peace,
until he spoke—smooth and fluid,
words free of accent,
yet carrying the weight of them all,
without accent.

Ameerah Shabazz
©2024

PAGE 36

Cuando Muejeres Hablan
When women speak
When women speak
Mujeres hablan

When women speak
We are reminded
kindness is not weakness

Hablamos de nuestra cultura, vida
de dondes nuestra espacio no dejan
articulate with more than voices

When women speak
whispers of wisdom tell
forgiveness does not erase the story

When women speak
actions of sacrifice,
moments of pain,
lifetimes of vulnerability,
lessons in defeats,
encouragement through victories

When WomenSpeak
bending - never breaking
Cuando mujeres hablan
Hablamos de nuetra corazones
Con tranquilidad y al paso
Hablmos con acción, passion y directamente

When Women speak
We hear a community of stillness
Give Voice to the silent
Embrace the wayward
Welcome your voice
In a universe of voices

When women speak
The language is based in love
Built on a foundation of lessons
Forced and created
Giving strength to otherwise ignored

When women speak
It takes a moment to articulate
That the echo we hear is the voice
Of those who speak back

Acknowledging and accepting
That when women speak
We are not alone
In this vast world of mothers, sisters, friends, daughters

When women speak
Our secrets are respected
Protected and eased

When women speak
We never speak alone

RescuePoetix | Susan Justiniano

Welcome to el barrioB
Previously Published in Brownstone Poets Anthology 2023

Welcome to el barrio!
where your dreams will seem to take flight all their own

Barrio dreams designed by rhythmic
salsa, merengue, bachata, bomba y plena

Barrio dreams spoken in dialects and laughter,
in Afro Latin cadence, filled with high rises and deep roots

Barrio dreams given birth in the gleam of ancestors,
in wide open spaces beyond the corner of your eye
where they fill every crevice of existence

Barrio dreams that seem impossible until they aren't,
given breath through will and determined callouses
breaking through blisters of expectations
living beyond the notion of freedom

Barrio dreams that sit dormant
but never die,
never starved by lack of imagination
or changes we can't control

Barrio dreams that possess the space
beyond the four blocks of streetlights
that show themselves at dusk,
heavy with the wings of memories

Barrio dreams that breathe beyond el barrio
to date to be free
where the smells of soul food bring you back
to the stories of youth

Welcome to el barrio,
where your dreams
begin in el tumbao of
everyday life

RescuePoetix | Susan Justiniano is a globally published, performing poet and twice-honored Poet Laureate. RescuePoetix™ professional artist brand was established in 2006 As a teaching artist and advocate she is deeply involved in the Arts globally, including active integration of the Arts through Social Justice and Education.
More info: https://linktr.ee/rescuepoetix

Lanea Collins
"Mi Corazón está en el Mundo"

"Mi Corazón está en el Mundo"
Traveling on the whispers howling through the midnight sky
The wind becomes her friend, the wind becomes her ride
The clouds become her pillow, making it safe to fly
As her anceSTARS guide her by their light

Dancing through the breeze as she spins and she spins
Her heart will be thumping to the melody of wind
Singing her heart out from the balcony, harmony finds her way
Through cobblestone paths, paved roads and dirt filled alleyways
Yes, harmony finds her way

Beating and beating to the beat of her own drum
Stomping her feet in the ground until she is numb
Lets her hair out loose just to shake it out
As she stands from the rooftop with her arms stretched out- she shouts
"Mi Corazón está en el Mundo"
This she knows without a doubt

She breaks bread and eats with the villagers until her heart is full
Cracks coconuts and cacao beans learning about culture
It's the rhythm of the people, the laughter in the air
She sees it in their eyes and how much they really care

She feels it in her bones when she listens to guitar
Learning the myths and stories of the lands from afar
Where I go she goes, hand in hand
She runs her fingers through the sand

She plays games and cracks jokes as she runs in the streets
Her shadow has awakened as she hides and she seeks
This is the gold that is buried down deep
She'd been searching for years to realize it was only skin deep
"Mi Corazón está en el Mundo"

She reminds herself to sleep
Where will she go next as she lays down to dream?
She writes down her journey and everything in between
Guided by the moon, it's in her heart that she sees

So she dreams and she dreams and she dreams and she dreams...

She dreams of smoking cigars while riding around in fancy cars
She dreams of being in colorful broke down stone buildings filled with nothing but feelings

Dreaming of her heart to be free like a dove
So she dreams of beautiful art as she is surrounded by love

So she pauses for a moment to look at her two feet
Where she finds herself today is where she is supposed to be
"Mi Corazón está en el Mundo"
"My heart is in the world"
So she leaves her heart is places that she truly does adore
And where she goes, her heart follows, all around the world
"Mi Corazón está en el Mundo"
"My heart is in the world"

Lanea Collins, educator and advocate of the arts, is the Creative Director of The Teaching Artist Hub CT.
Lanea has performed in various productions. She is a Goodwin College award winning poet of, and is the writer, speaker and author of "My Heart Is Art", a certified arts trainer in the principles of nonviolence.

<u>Awaken child</u>

Time to rise

Open my eyes

to a new beginning

A fresh start

But first don't miss the mark

Don't miss the chance to give thanks

For placing me in places I didn't want to be

For challenging me to open up with sincerity

To stop running from my heart's vulnerability

So that I could see the light and love in me clearly

La Negra Tiene Tumbao

I wanted to place these words

with care

and without complications

and in full acceptance

That I no longer have to live

in the deficit of the world's definition of black

That depression will no longer darken my doorsteps

That traumatic memories will no longer rain clouds on my parade

That when I open my eyes

they now reflect the beauty in honoring the balance of God's scales

That my faith will stabilize my soul

Al que madruga Dios lo ayuda

I honor the silence of His voice in the quiet hours of sunrise

As I believe the sun does

Taking its time to crest over our nesting natures

Dancing across the treetops while it tickles the clouds to wake up

Everything now in full essence of color

PAGE 41

This world is so vast yet

We are so intricately united with each other

And that knowledge empowers her

La Negra Tiene Tumbao

She is the embodiment of her community

Her people's heartstring

She is on her feet in full praise

Dancing to the song of second chances

With the Sun

With her purpose

She is light and love

As she dances in red

Her hips as crimson ribbons

He aura is golden against the warmth

of her copper skin

And she loved herself

as a rainbow

Evonda Thomas
Poetyss is a New Jersey based poet/writer and graduate of Rutgers University. She enjoys hosting and curating events as co-owner of The Meraki Collective. She's a member of When Women Speak, Honeydrippers Poetry Collective and the Don Evans Players. Follow her at im_poetyss

Cigar Ladies in Cuba

Her leg crossed heavy-like
relaxed cool tired like
Don't give a fuck like
Cigar in hand
with piano fingers
I got my shit right
unbothered
Boss lady layered-like
Sexy cocky grown-like
Cowboy hood chick lean-like
thin thighs coffee bean brown
Eyes smokey pretty flirty right
Afro braided locd
Blowing smoke sitting
all at home-like
up in Cuba barns and stoops
wit fine wine swag right
Glowing in slow lanes nice-like

Spanish Version

Mujeres de los Puros en Cuba
Su pierna cruzada pesada
relajada, fresca, cansada
Sin preocupaciones
con un puro en la mano
y dedos de pianista.
Tengo todo en orden,
sin molestias,
Dama de negocios, con estilo.
Sexy, segura, adulta,
chica del campo, relajada,
muslos delgados, color café.
Ojos ahumados, coquetos, bellos,
trenzas afros, locs,
exhalando humo, sentada
como en casa,
en los graneros y escalones de Cuba,
con una copa de vino elegante,
brillando en calles lentas, con gracia.

**Enfield, CT. Poet Laureate
Nzima Hutchings**

Nzima is the Poet Laureate of Enfield, Connecticut (2023-2025) and a master teaching artist, literary art wellness trainer, and coach. As a certified leader with Amherst Writers & Artists, she leads workshops and retreats that foster creativity and self-expression in holistic settings. A best-selling author, Nzima is the visionary founder of Hartford's Literary Integrated Trailblazers (Hartford's L.I.T.) and the Hartford Book Festival, enriching Greater Hartford's cultural landscape. She also hosts an annual writing retreat for women, is the founder of LAWR Magazine, and hosts the Nzima Poetry Cafe Show on Cox Studios, promoting poetic art and community engagement.

Piano Lady New Claim

Her tears revealed a new claiming; ancestors' cries of joy soaked her and the streets like rain, like the echoes of lacquered black piano notes, that played loudly in Havana's streets, welcoming Assata Shakur. Like the way Celia Cruz song Azucar soaked airwaves, the way Nina Simone piano cried for more, and claimed needing more sugar in her bowl, filling souls. She is no longer a sideshow, an onlooker in the theater of life. Like the lady wearing a faded red, nearly pink dress, shaking snow globes in secondhand stores, watching worlds swirl in glasses of water, too afraid to live outside and get wet, each scene a frozen moment, a quiet echo of existence.

In her beginnings of her becoming, the Orisha maracas had shaken, as if God had spoken, summoning all the women she was, she is, to speak, to meet, to retreat, to just be. Her hands moved frantically wobbling and stumbling like a chicken with his head cut off bopping up and down on every ivory and black keys. A place she let loose, in solitude to figure it out.

She started strumming her pain, *strumming her pain with her fingers, seeing her life in the world— things that killed her softly for so long, killing her softly.*

Turning her brown dress red, rojo, like aged wine, sangria, like the lady of the night, from Spanish Harlem, the kind men say *"nice to meet you," "Mucho Gusto"* silkening her flesh and bones, something she never fathomed. Flowers all turned yellow in her space, it be her inner longings folded in the air, her being a woman outside now story. Her reveal dangles like citrine crystal earrings on trees; ethereal like. In spite of her shortcomings, loss and her imperfections, she managed to be a blessin.

She can't take back yesterday's moments when her heart hunted for the love space demands, when her mind was stunted, arrested in development and she played touch and go with vices.

She's at home with herself now, no longer a guest tiptoeing in someone else's house, she wore her red dress and her new soul, an invitation to her ceremonious renaming.

She owns being the teeth and tongues in red, brown, and burgundy thick lipped mouths, the arch in the mahogany, the amber-brown, blue-black, the redbone backs. She came from the women who played endlessly on life's rhythmic keys. Some in and out of tune, unique in stock, from the yellowish to reddish wombs of many, a million moons ago— never to be forgot.

She claims being Every Kinda Lady too, the kind she gotta be… for the ones she will never meet. As she plays on in these mean streets.

Nzima Hutchings

Patria o Muerte

When I was naive, I was taught not to like anyone who is communist.

When I was in High School I learned about the Cold War, Bay of Pigs, and the Cuban Missile Crisis.

When I was in College I was taught Cuba was the enemy of the American Government.

When I did not swallow what I was spoon fed, I discovered Cuba and Puerto Rico are beautiful Caribbean islands that have much more in common.

Puerto Rico is the oldest colony of the world.

Boricuas have been oppressed, repressed, and colonized for more than 500 years. First by Spain, and then the United States.

As a former colony, Cuba understands the pain of my people and is not afraid to speak up about it. Cuba's 1978 Policy on Puerto Rico is evidence of this.

Fidel Castro loved and supported Puerto Rico. As the leader of Cuba he fought for Independence. He wanted the same for el Borinquen..

Castro was very much like our leader Pedro Albizu Campos. They were two gandules in a pod.

Albizu studied law at Harvard College, and Castro at the University of Habana. Both leaders formed organizations dedicated to fight for liberation.

Albizu was the President of the Nationalist Party

in Puerto Rico, and the leader of the Independence Movement. Castro founded the 26th of July Movement to overthrow the Trujillo government.

Albizu and Castro were revolutionaries who believed en la Patria's ability to self determine.

Both were knowledgeable men who used their wisdom to fight the power.

Albizu inspired many leaders including Castro, Che Guevarra, and Malcolm X. He wrote the Irish Constitution with James Connoly and inspired the

Irish War of Independence. Castro inspired the Cuban Revolution.

Both men were persecuted because of their anti colonial stance. Albizu was imprisoned and tortured in La Princessa until his death. Castro was imprisoned in the Presidio Modelo until released.

Darlene Elias

Darlene Elias is an emerging writer and poet from Western Mass. She is a Hawaiian Boricua Anti Colonial Feminist who uses literature, poetry, and spoken word to elevate and validate her own experiences as a woman who is part of the diaspora in the U.S. She lives in Holyoke, a sister pueblo of Puerto Rico, with her partner and dogs.

BAUTISMO (BAPTISM)

Strongly embrace me, Red River.

Enwrap me with your shawl.

Sweet arms, fortunate blood,

Body and spirit completely.

My body for sacred red clothes -

Envelop me in your robe and

Red shawl of your unique soul -

Mami Wata, Mother of Africa,

Mami Wata, my hands and crown.

Embrace me - I am your red daughter.

Devotion with my heart and mouth.

Proud of my Caribbean mocha skin.

My life is the light and shadow.

I sing, dance, always returning to the sea

Creating magic with our waters.

Strongly embrace me, Mother of All Waters.

Enwrap me with your treasure shawl.

Sweet arms, fortunate blood,

Body and soul totally.

My body for sacred red clothes.

Envelop me in your robe.

Envelop me in your robe.

Envelop me...

Abrazame fuerte Rio rojo.

Tápame con tu rebozo.

Brazos dulce, sangre suerte,

Cuerpo y espíritu totalmente.

Cuerpo mio por ropa roja divina,

Envuélvame en tu túnica y

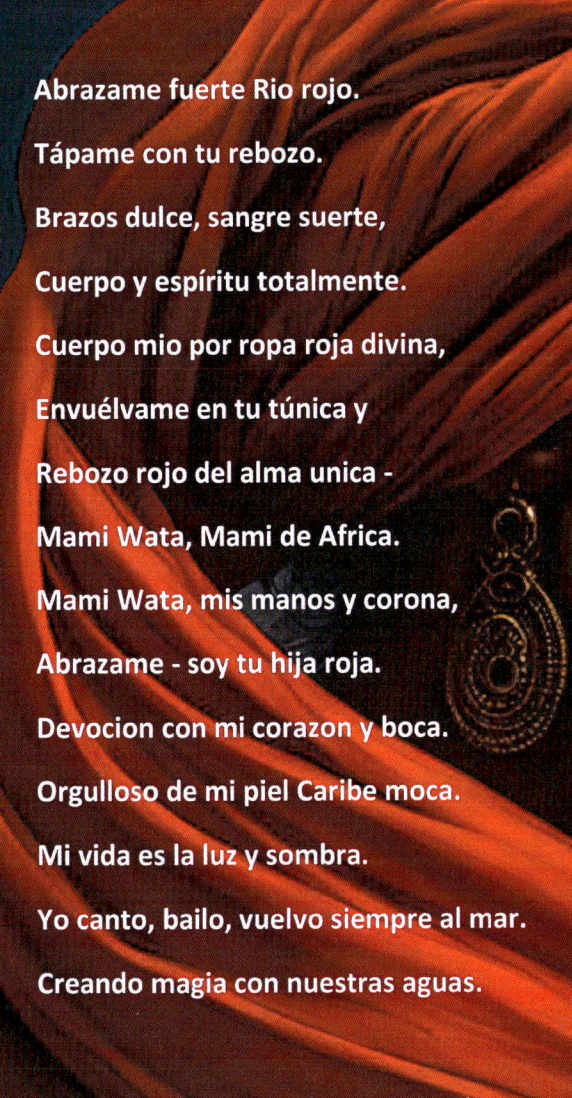

Rebozo rojo del alma unica -

Mami Wata, Mami de Africa.

Mami Wata, mis manos y corona,

Abrazame - soy tu hija roja.

Devocion con mi corazon y boca.

Orgulloso de mi piel Caribe moca.

Mi vida es la luz y sombra.

Yo canto, bailo, vuelvo siempre al mar.

Creando magia con nuestras aguas.

Abrazame fuerte Madre aguas todos.

Tapame con tu rebozo tesoro.

Brazos dulce, sangre suerte,

Cuerpo y alma totalmente.

Cuerpo mio por ropa rojo divina,

Envuélveme en tu túnica.

Envuélveme en tu túnica.

Envuélveme…

© 2024 Queen Mother Imakhu (Elaine Lloyd-Nazario

"La Sirena" Queen Mother Imakhu has enjoyed a fifty-year professional career in the arts. Singer, songwriter, poet, storyteller, musician, dancer, filmmaker, multimedia producer, and yogini. Enstooled/initiated Khametic Queen Mother, Bantu nganga, and Interfaith Minister. Founder of Blacknificently LatinX Media. Queen Mother Imakhu believes, "Art heals the world."

Death of white supremacy- eulogy

By Gri Saex

We burry you today!

And with you we burry your **hypocrisy,**

Your sicken soul,

The deep pain you never got over,

Your twisted ideas that **tortured** you and us,

The patriarchal system you choose to follow all of your life.

And let's be **clear** that,

You left behind a legacy of inconceivable acts

Harmful, corrupt, and unjust laws we must **not** forget

and must **carve** in the next chapters of our history

for your children, our children, and their successors **not to repeat.**

Go down now as your contorted body, like a tornado

descends into the deep holes of mother earth,

where you will **submi**t and **accept** as your new dwelling

for all eternity.

Dead is all you are now!

Powers surrendered

No more suffering and desperation

But **reparations /reparations/reparations**

Go and perhaps you will emerge fallen eagle

with new wings

made of love and heart

song (traditionally sung at funerals)

"Adios con el Corazon/que con el alma no puedo/ al despedirme de ti/ De sentimientos **no** muero/ tu seras el **mal** de mi vida/ tu seras el pajaro pinto que ya no canta por las mananas!"

Go now rest in peace! white supremacy!

White supremacy (Spanish Version)

white supremacy te sepultamos hoy

y contigo enterramos

 tu hiprocresia

tu alma enferma!

el dolor profundo que no superaste

las ideas trajiversadas que a menudo te torturaron y nos

torturaron

el sistema patriarchal y destructivo al que escojiste seguir toda tu vida

pero que quede claro

que dejaste un legado de actos inconcebibles

y leyes corruptas, daninas e injustas que no podemos

olvidar

y las tallaremos en tu capitulo final hoy!

Para que nuestros hijos y sus sucesivos no repitan tus

atrocidades

white supremacy

Vete

Y que tu cuerpo contorcionado como un tornado

descienda a las cavernas profundas de la madre tierra

ante la cual

has de fundirte y rendirte derrotado

aceptandola como tu nueva morada

por toda la eternidad!

Acepta tu captura y descomposicion

Renuncia y claudica tu existencia

Dejando ese pasado horroroso atras,

Entrega todo lo que fuiste

y entregate al amor y la

sanacion!

Canto: adios con el Corazon que con el alma no puedo /al despedirme de ti de sentimientos NO muero./ Tu seras el mal que hoy dejamos,/ tu seras el aguila fallida que hoy enterramos

Entrega tus alas llacences en las llamas ardiente

aguila vencida

Y vuelve al suelo al cual estas condenada

Y tal vez renaceras con nuevas alas,

con Corazon,

y libre de las impurezas del pasado.

Regresa a la luz

y la belleza

Y tal vez renaceras

trayendo **justicia y libertad**!

Por ahora descansa en paz!

Gri Saex, originally from the Dominican Republic, is a budding artist and community advocate in Springfield, MA. A recipient of the 2022 Marty Nathan Art and Activism grant, she's a founding member of Somos Semillas, attended the Clemente Program, and currently studies at Bard College while serving on the board of A Queens Narrative and in the leadership of Survival Theater Project.

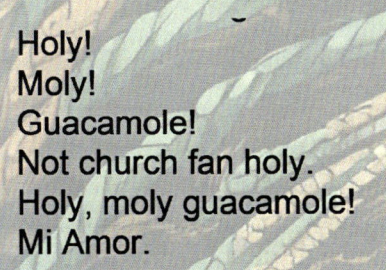

Holy!
Moly!
Guacamole!
Not church fan holy.
Holy, moly guacamole!
Mi Amor.

She's everything nice
But with a whole lotta spice!
Sugar *and* spice?
Mmmm…
She's spicy hot,
And as cold as ice!
Mi Amor.

She's ripe green
Like granny smith.
Candy green,
Candied yams.
Candy green *and* sweet yams?
Mi AMor

She's every man's dream,
Every girl's bestie.
Never messy!
Nor will she stress thee.
Mi Amor

She's like bright yellow sunshine.
She *is* sunshine!
The color of sunshine,
Bright yellow,
Like ripe, ready, robust bananas!
Mi Amor

Ready to be ravished.
Yellow bananas
Long, firm, sweet, kinda hard,
But soft on the tongue.
Mi Amor

She's strong, driven, juicy.
Radiant and radical, like red!
Red like cherries.

Mi Amor

Mi Amor
I really love you!
I've lived long enough
Realizing how amazingly delicious
You are to me and to the world.
The world craves you!
The raw, pure, organic, unbothered you!

Mi Amor
With your nurturing qualities,
You've fed me.
You've filled me.
You feed me,
Goodness and wellness,
All my life!

Mi Amor
Now I promise to love you,
Enjoy you!
Grow you!
Cultivate you!
For the rest of my life!
Mi Amor
Te Amo!

Nadine Nicola Green

Nadine Nicola Green, LCSW, is dedicated to empowering others on their self-help journeys. As the founder and CEO of Access GREENADINE LLC, she offers clients access to Growth, Resilience, Empowerment, and Elevation. With degrees in Psychology and Social Work from the University of Connecticut, Nadine has extensive experience working with diverse groups, including children, families, at-risk youth, and BIPOC communities. She is also a devoted mother, wellness coach, speaker, best-selling author, and advocate for spiritual alignment.

She moves like fire wrapped in silk—a crimson flame

Flames against the darkening sky.

Red and clinging whispering woes away.

Fire of the dress gives power to her soul.

Red clings and sways, whispering secrets to the wind.

Bare feet kiss the earth, marking rhythm like waves to shores.

Steel drums coil around her, sweet and wild,

Which beat is the drum and which is her heart?

Each spin sends the fringe of the hem edges flying,

Scarlet blur igniting the night. She and the dress dance

To the beat of freedom, hips sway mixing the brew of magic.

Cha-cha - Danzón married to steel drums, a veil of red.

A drum beat rumbles through heart in sync

Caught in warm island breezes - mixed with love and sun warmth.

Stars lean close, lamps leave the sky

Spewing red fire flares enough to dye the fabric of dress and life.

Entranced and drawn by the heat of motion and the brilliance of red

Sweat beads bend and bow making streams on cheeks.

Streams glow like hibiscus petals beneath moonlight.

In the heart of the dance, salsa, mambo! Ayee!

She is not just a woman in a red dress—

No, she is fire and ice - life.

She is a force, a spirit, a living song descendant of Yoruba.

Red blood of the island - once floated next to its mother's womb,

Placenta wrapped, umbilical cord in place - tethered

Swaying to the eternal rhythm of life.

In the sultry twilight of a Caribbean night,

She moves like fire wrapped in silk—a crimson flame.

Oh what a dance, red feet, red dance, red fire

A red-dressed woman - feeder of the flame.

©2024 Ameerah Shabazz-Bilal

PAGE 53

Dear Black Woman,

Dear Black Woman

I wish for you what I never found.

Unconditional love and support.

Grace under fire.

And the time to rest,   and do nothing.

Oh, the burdens of being extraordinary.

24/7   365 days   Five hundred   Twenty-five thousand   Nine hundred   and twenty-nine   point two seconds.

Every year,   since conception.

While looking   this   fabulous.

Weighs more than the weight

of snow on branches

or George Floyd's last breath.

The moon nor the heavens

combined are worthy of the quiet dignity

our mothers   and mothers before them,   bored into their pride for survival's sake.

They were the blueprints. for walking on water,   unconditional love   and sacrifice.

Their ancestral spirts were not broken at

 Curacaco   Puerto Rico   Haiti   The Dominican Republic   Cuba

    or any of the islands that severed as a breading farm,

      for Black gold trafficked to the Americas.

Dear Black Woman,   I see you,   like I see me.

        Worthy. Deserving. Educated. Powerful. Dynamic. A blessing.

You are not heavy, you are my HERstory.

Through trauma and history   Through slave dungeons and cotton fields.

Through picket lines and double standards.

Through *The Color Purple* and *Waiting To Exhale*.

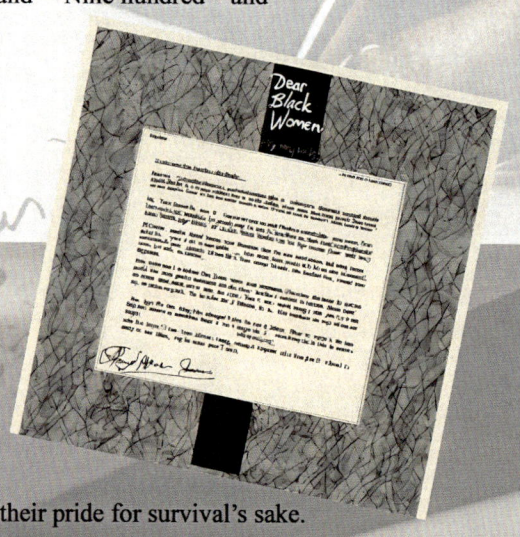

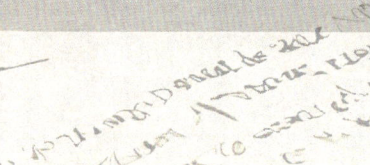

PAGE 54

Through tears and pain.

Dear Black Woman, My double X chromosome warrior goddess.

That song, *"Never Should Have Made It"* sings differently to me now.

Knowing our lips and mouths were burned.

So, we could slowly starve to death.

As a warning for others to behave or suffer the consequences.

But we have never been afraid of good trouble.

Never should have made it,

never should have made it,

Never Should have made it.

Dear Black Woman, I see you. Like me.

Still fighting the same fights to be seen to be heard to be more than three fifths.

Say her name like,

    Sandra Bland   Dr. Cadi- Bailey   Azura Banks   Julia Griffin

Say YOUR name

With the hopes that somewhere on the road to the future

Despair will be a footnote about this day.

A Thursday.

The day that we summoned the strength.

The courage, the wit, the knowledge to guide us out of the darkness of separation

towards the covenant of sisterhood.

Knowing, like Emmett's mother Sometimes caskets must be kept open.

Dear Black Women, I see you And I wish for you what I never found.

The time to rest and do nothing…

Helena D. Lewis

When Women Speak / *Every Kinda Lady*
Poetic Writing Prompt by Nzima Hutchings

Instructions:
Fill in the Blanks: Consider the qualities, feelings, memories, and identities that resonate with you or with women you admire. Use vivid metaphors, cultural descriptors, and empowering, edgy language to fill in each blank with words or phrases that encapsulate these ideas.

Reflect: Once you've completed your poem, write a brief paragraph about your choices. What do these words convey about women? How do they capture the essence of women's voices and experiences?

Share: If you're comfortable, share your finished poem and reflection with the group. Engage in a discussion about the diverse experiences and expressions of women that surfaced in your writing.

Example Poem:
When women speak, she echoes every kinda lady: "I am from stories."
When women speak, the lady wearing a crown of wildflowers and screaming into voids,
She suddenly remembers she is a warrior and where she is from.
She is from the rhythm of her ancestors' tongues, teeth, and warm womb desires.
When women speak, every kinda lady dances with fire...

Start here (extra paper may be needed)

When women speak, she echoes every kinda lady: "I am from stories."

When women speak, the lady wearing _____ and screaming _____ She suddenly remembers she is _____ _____ and where she is from. _____. When women speak, every kinda lady _____ _____ _____ When women speak, she _____ and _____ then _____ _____ _____ _____ _____ and _____ When women speak _____ _____ She becomes _____ _____ and her voice _____ every kinda lady.

PAGE 56

In a world where imports and exports don't shake hearts or hands,
We lean on the human spirit, the ingenuity of antiques,
Where classics whisper tales of old-fashioned love,
And the beauty of antiquity cradles our souls.
Making poor and mismatched moments clever and rich.

Nzima Hutchings

Photo Credit: Barbara McClane

"THE TRUTH OF THE MATTER IS THAT STORIES NEVER DIE. SOMEONE OR SOMETHING HOLDS THE MEMORIES AND KNOWS OF THE JOURNEY."

QUOTE BY: NZIMA HUTCHINGS

"LA VERDAD ES QUE LAS HISTORIAS NUNCA MUEREN. ALGUIEN O ALGO GUARDA LOS RECUERDOS Y CONOCE EL VIAJE."

PAGE 58

Photo Credit Ameerah Shabazz - Bilal

Pedal On

In spite of
the powers that be,
long wrath & debris
alongside tourists'
judging postures
neck bends
mixed with emotions
bits of pity, fascination
bulging eyes
and all the admirations
tucked in the folds
of disbelieving brows
trigger fingers
clicking buttons
and the foreign dialects
and languages
echoing in backgrounds

"I got the picture"
tengo la foto

we be the side show
"Photos don't lie"

not angry
just knowingly

in spite of
onlookers watching
cradling souls
in embrace,
content in their
wandering,
and our figuring it out,

Nosotros pedaleamos en
we pedal on

we pedal on
pushing
finishing up on with
the day to day
the mundane
surviving and
living

Nzima Hutchings

PAGE 59

Every Kinda Lady
Anthropological Tongue
Vignette Writing Exercise

Infusing an "anthropological tongue" into creative writing empowers writers to deepen authenticity and craft an immersive experience that captivates readers. This unique approach breathes life into narratives, weaving intricate cultural details and nuanced perspectives that invite audiences to explore worlds beyond their own. By harnessing this vibrant linguistic style, writers can transform their storytelling into a vivid tapestry, enriching both characters and settings while drawing readers into a profound, engaging journey.

In creative writing, preserving this authenticity benefits writers and readers by:

1. Cultural Representation: It allows diverse cultures and backgrounds to be accurately portrayed, enriching the narrative with unique voices and experiences.

2. Realism and Connection: Maintaining the real speech patterns and vocabulary of characters creates a stronger emotional connection for readers, making the story feel more genuine and relatable.

3. Vibrant Characters: Characters feel more alive and distinct when their language is grounded in real-world expressions and dialects.

4. Creative Exploration: Writers can explore different ways of storytelling through the diverse voices and expressions of their characters, adding depth and complexity to the narrative.

5. Respect for Heritage: It honors the origins and traditions of the people or communities being written about, fostering respect and understanding of their heritage.

6. Exposition: This is the beginning of the story where the setting, characters, and background information are introduced. It sets the stage for the narrative and provides essential context. Stay true to the setting, characters when setting the stage. Do the research, be fearless, write what you know.

These definitions lay the foundation for understanding how maintaining the "integrity of verbiage" means preserving the authenticity and truth of how real people speak and express themselves within a cultural or artistic context, respecting their voice and experiences. "Anthropological tongue" refers to preserving the authentic language, culture, and voice of real people in creative writing. This concept emphasizes staying true to how people naturally speak and express themselves, ensuring the integrity of their words and experiences is maintained.

Anthropologist:
An anthropologist is a scholar who studies human societies, cultures, and their development. Their work often includes examining the ways people interact within their cultural and social environments, as well as how these contexts shape language, customs, beliefs, and behaviors.

Voice:
In literature, *voice* refers to the distinctive style or tone of an author or narrator that conveys personality, perspective, and emotion. It is the unique quality that allows the reader to "hear" the writer's or character's presence. This can include word choice, sentence structure, rhythm, and point of view.

Integrity:
Integrity refers to the quality of being honest and having strong moral principles. In a literary or artistic context, it involves maintaining authenticity, consistency, and a true representation of the subject matter without compromising values or misrepresenting the voices and experiences of others.

Vignette: is a short, descriptive scene or snapshot that captures a moment, idea, or character. It often focuses on a specific detail or emotion, creating a vivid impression without telling a complete story.

<u>Instructions</u>

Grab a notebook and dive into a whirlwind of creativity! In just 15 minutes, craft a story or vignette bursting with unapologetic anthropological flair. Let your words flow freely, embracing the vibrant tapestry of human experience.

When the timer goes off, take a moment to reflect. How does it feel to have woven your thoughts into a narrative? Are you invigorated by the raw expression of culture and identity? Did any unexpected emotions surface as you explored this creative landscape? Celebrate the journey of creation, no matter where it takes you!

Assata Shakur

Assata Shakur's Quotes

Read and respond to the quotes below. Next, write a letter on a separate sheet of paper to her as if you knew she would be reading it.

The quote "I am not a criminal. I am a revolutionary" reflects Assata Shakur's perspective on her identity and activism. She made this statement during her time in Cuba, specifically in the late 1980s and early 1990s after she was granted asylum there.

Assata had been a prominent figure in the Black Panther Party and the Black Liberation Army in the 1970s, and her activism led to her being charged with various crimes, including the killing of a state trooper—a charge she denied and viewed as politically motivated. After escaping from prison in 1979, she fled to Cuba, where she continued to speak out against racial injustice and systemic oppression.

This declaration emphasizes her self-identification as a revolutionary, challenging the labels imposed on her by the state and asserting her commitment to the broader struggle for liberation and social justice.

Assata Shakur made several notable statements while in Cuba that reflect her views on freedom, resistance, and solidarity.

1. I am a Black woman, and I want to be free."

2. "The struggle is a constant thing. You cannot win the struggle if you do not put your life on the line."

3. "I am not a criminal. I am a revolutionary"

Letter to Assata Shakur

Dear Assata,

I hope this message reaches you. Your powerful words and unwavering commitment to justice continue to inspire many, including me. Your declaration, "I am not a criminal. I am a revolutionary," resonates deeply as it challenges how society defines activism. It's a reminder that fighting for freedom is a noble cause, even in the face of adversity.

Your courage in standing up against oppression motivates us to do the same in our communities. Thank you for your resilience and for paving the way for future generations. Your legacy is a testament to the power of hope and the importance of standing firm in our beliefs.

In solidarity,
A Sister hoping to meet you
Every Kinda Lady N

Junk Journaling

Junk journaling is a creative form of journaling that utilizes a mix of materials, scraps, and artistic mediums. This practice encourages mindfulness, relaxation, and creativity. The reason why junk journaling is an act of mindfulness, is because it requires you to be fully present in the moment, focusing only on creativity. It can also serve as a muse for creative writing or oral storytelling, inspiring vivid imagery and imaginative worlds. Through junk journaling, individuals can embrace different time periods, the beginning of a romance novel, fantasy fiction, or even a gripping mystery and give new life to everyday items like old books, magazines, and jewelry, transforming them into art. It's a wonderful way to repurpose and reimagine the ordinary, fostering both personal expression and. environmental mindfulness.

How to Start Junk Journaling:

1. Gather Materials:
   Collect scraps such as old books, magazines, postcards, wrapping paper, fabric scraps, broken jewelry, beads, keys, stickers, etc. You can use almost anything—your goal is to repurpose items creatively.
   - You'll also need a journal or notebook as your base, along with glue, tape, scissors, markers, and pens.

2. Choose a Theme or Focus:
   - Decide if your junk journal will follow a specific theme, like fantasy, romance, or travel, or let it be spontaneous.
   - Themes can help guide the visuals and inspire creative writing.

3. Arrange and Layer:
   - Layer your materials by gluing or taping them onto pages. Arrange things freely—don't worry about perfection.
   - Mix textures and colors to create visual interest. For example, use fabric scraps with torn pages from an old book or colorful magazine clippings.

4. Incorporate Writing Prompts:
   - As you glue and arrange, jot down keywords, phrases, or sentences inspired by the visuals.
   - Use your materials to prompt creative writing ideas. For example, an old photograph could inspire a historical story, or torn pages from a sci-fi magazine could lead to a futuristic plot.

5. Write in Your Junk Journal:
   - Begin writing on the decorated pages. Use the textures, images, and items you've included to guide your creativity.
   - You can start small with phrases, lists, or descriptions that connect to what you've pasted down.

Junk Journals | Creative Writing and Mindfulness

Writing Prompts from Your Junk Journal

Observe the Page:
Look at your finished junk journal page. What jumps out at you? Is it a particular image, color, or material? Allow that to spark a story or idea.

Write a Character or Scene
Imagine the people or places that fit into the mood or visuals on the page. Write a brief character description or start a scene:

Example:
If you pasted an old key onto the page, you could write:
"The rusty key had been forgotten for years in the attic, but when Tatiana found it, she knew it was more than just a trinket. It held the secret to a door she'd been warned never to open."

Expand the Story:
Use the initial character or scene to create a larger piece. Is it the beginning of a mystery or a romance? Keep building the story, letting the journal elements inspire further details.
By combining journaling with writing, you create both visual art and a story, making the process immersive and freeing.

Junk Journaling | Creative Writing | Traveling

Junk journaling and creative writing become especially exciting when traveling. As you experience new places and cultures, you can incorporate those details into your visual or literary work. Challenge yourself by purchasing something small from a local gift shop or gathering meaningful items from your surroundings—like a ticket stub, a pressed flower, a seashell or a unique piece of fabric. These small treasures will add depth and personal significance to your journal, allowing you to reflect the essence of the places you've visited and the moments you've encountered.

Junk Journals

PAGE 67

Evocative Writing

How to Write an Evocative Creative Writing Piece
IMAGERY
"Put your pearls down for 1 minute"

**Read. Add Your Spin.
Grow Outside Your Comforts...**

Example: (excerpt from Black Frida)
 by Nzima Hutchings ©2023 Black Frida

    Roach spray, burnt popcorn, and the smell of all-day-long sex filled the room. My "Who dat is, Harpo?" eyes traced and swept wildly around the raggedy room, just like her legs and arms wrapped around his back. It was in that moment I stood outside myself, almost losing all I had left. But I stayed sneaky-cat quiet like, staying there watching like a voyeur, a freak getting off, excited. I decided then and there—I'll leave when I'm ready. Not empty-handed.

"She moaned, 'Oh Escobar, oh Escobar,' like an annoying, mental hurt parrot. He called her his Black Frida; my soul side-eyed the mutha f*cker real hard and cried too... that's what he called me."

 I nearly lost it in that moment. The chipped teal and antique white walls looked even more cracked, exposing every flaw. The tear and cigarette-burned hole in that old, crushed velvet sad brown couch looked extra pitiful. I pitied myself for falling for the illusion of vintage art, the lie of a struggling artist's love. It was false, and I had mistaken the cracks for character.

The avocado metal-bladed fan, the kind that'll cut ya finger off, rocked in the window, with a ticking sound slicing through the thick air, while "Aye poppy, lil mommy, I ain't no punta" echoed in the background, blending with the sirens and the ice cream truck's jingle. I still hear the ticking and it all. It feels like it's in HD, sharp and coming for me. It's strange, the things you remember when you're sitting all alone behind bars. Here I am, holding a pretty well-made makeshift dildo that even looks like a real dick, with nothing but time to think about how I got here—and those haunting sounds to keep me company.

EVOCATIVE WRITING

1. Focus on Emotion
Start by deciding what emotions you want to evoke in your readers. Let those feelings guide your tone, characters, and setting. Writing is most powerful when it resonates emotionally.

2. Use Vivid Sensory Details
Engage your reader's senses by describing more than just what they see. What does your scene smell like? What sounds are in the background? Vivid details make your story feel real.

3. Step Outside the Box
To write something memorable, you must take risks. Push your boundaries, experiment with new genres, or approach your story in unconventional ways. Writing in a space that feels unfamiliar can lead to creative breakthroughs.

4. Leave Your Comfort Zone
Writing evocatively often requires stepping into the shoes of characters or exploring themes outside of your experience. Doing this stretches your empathy and helps you write more deeply layered characters.

5. Separate Yourself from Your Characters
Give your characters their own voice. Avoid making them mirrors of yourself. Let them have unique flaws, desires, and conflicts. This makes them feel real and relatable to readers.

6. Show, Don't Tell
Instead of stating how a character feels, show it through their actions or body language. This makes the writing more immersive and engaging.

7. Embrace Symbolism and Metaphor
Metaphors and symbols add depth and help readers connect emotionally with your story. Use them to convey themes and emotions in a subtle but powerful way.

8. Write Authentically
Even in fiction, authenticity matters. Let the emotions and motivations of your characters come from a real place. Readers connect most with writing that feels genuine.

Why It's Important to Step Outside Your Comfort Zone:
Writing outside your comfort zone allows you to explore ideas, perspectives, and experiences you might never encounter in your daily life. It forces growth, both as a writer and a person. Characters born from this place of discomfort will often feel more authentic, and your readers will appreciate the depth. Writing from new and challenging perspectives leads to innovative storytelling, fostering creativity and pushing the boundaries of your craft.

Why You Must Separate Yourself from Your Characters:
The characters you create should have their own distinct voices, desires, and motivations. If you project too much of yourself into a character, you risk limiting their potential. By giving your characters space to develop independently, you create a more complex and rich narrative that readers can relate to, even if the character's experiences differ from their own. This separation allows you to explore human emotions and situations more fully and without bias, making your writing more dynamic and universal.

Writing evocatively requires fearlessness—pushing beyond what feels safe and easy to create something raw, real, and unforgettable. When you challenge yourself as a writer, you elevate your craft and captivate your readers. So, dare to step outside the box and watch your stories come to life.

Nzima Hutchings, the author of "Black Frida", describes herself as authentic and a risk-taker, yet she had never used the word "dick" or " mental" in her work before, which pushed her further out of her literary comfort zone.

Here's why it's evocative:

Sensory Details: The description of smells, sounds, and visuals (roach spray, the moans, the cracked walls) engages the senses and immerses the reader in the atmosphere.

Emotional Depth: The narrator's feelings of loss, betrayal, and self-pity are palpable, allowing readers to connect emotionally with the character's experience.

Imagery: The vivid descriptions of the surroundings, like the "avocado metal-bladed fan" and the "old, crushed velvet sad brown couch," create a strong visual impression and convey the setting's decay.

Internal Reflection: The narrator's introspection, especially in moments of watching and feeling like a voyeur, adds a layer of complexity to the emotional landscape.

Top View Writing Prompt

Setting the Scene:
Find yourself at a height—whether on a rooftop, treetop, mountain top, or even a balcony. Imagine you have a bird's-eye view of the world below. Take a moment to soak in your surroundings.

Look Around:
Gaze out and trace the area carefully with your eyes. Take in the elements: the colors, the shapes, the movement. Snap a mental picture of this scene and store it in your mind's eye.

Listen:
Close your eyes for one minute. Focus on the sounds around you—the rustle of leaves, distant voices, the hum of the city, or the whisper of the wind. Let these sounds fill your awareness.

Write:
Now, grab your pen and paper. Write non-stop in a stream of consciousness for five minutes. Let your thoughts flow freely, capturing the sensations, reflections, and emotions that arise. Don't worry about structure or grammar—just let it pour out.

Reflect:
After you finish writing, take a moment to reflect on the experience:
What did you notice that you might have overlooked before?
Did you feel bigger and more powerful, or smaller and more connected?
Did feelings of a God-like complex or judgment creep in?

Make It Fun:
You can also try this activity in other heights—like a hot air balloon or a Ferris wheel!

Benefits
This exercise fosters mindfulness, enhances your observational skills, and cultivates gratitude while creating a rich setting for your stories. Enjoy the experience and see where your thoughts take you!
Be safe!!

When Women Speak

	NOTES

	NOTES

	NOTES

PAGE 72

LAWR TEN-POINT GOALS

AMPLIFY VOICES: CREATE A PLATFORM FOR WOMEN TO SHARE THEIR STORIES AND PERSPECTIVES, ENSURING DIVERSE VOICES ARE HEARD AND CELEBRATED.

FOSTER WELLNESS: PROMOTE PRACTICES AND RESOURCES THAT SUPPORT HOLISTIC WELL-BEING, ENCOURAGING MINDFULNESS AND SELF-CARE THROUGH CREATIVE EXPRESSION.

ENCOURAGE CREATIVITY: INSPIRE WOMEN TO EXPLORE AND ENGAGE IN LITERARY AND VISUAL ARTS AS TOOLS FOR PERSONAL GROWTH AND HEALING.

BUILD COMMUNITY: CULTIVATE A SUPPORTIVE NETWORK OF WOMEN DEDICATED TO SHARING EXPERIENCES, COLLABORATING, AND UPLIFTING ONE ANOTHER.

CREATE LEGACY: ESTABLISH A RICH LITERARY ARCHIVE THAT HONORS WOMEN'S CONTRIBUTIONS AND STORIES, ENSURING THEIR IMPACT RESONATES FOR GENERATIONS TO COME.

EMBRACE RISK: ENCOURAGE WOMEN TO TAKE CREATIVE RISKS AND PRODUCE WORK FREE FROM SELF-JUDGMENT, FOSTERING AN ENVIRONMENT WHERE ALL EXPRESSIONS ARE WELCOMED.

CULTIVATE SELF-CONNECTION: SUPPORT WOMEN IN FORGING MEANINGFUL CONNECTIONS WITH THEMSELVES THROUGH INTROSPECTIVE PRACTICES AND CREATIVE EXPLORATION.

FOSTER AN ALCHEMIST MINDSET: INSPIRE WOMEN TO TRANSFORM PERSONAL EXPERIENCES INTO POWERFUL STORIES AND ART THAT RESONATE WITH OTHERS.

CELEBRATE DIVERSITY: WELCOME AND UPLIFT EVERY KIND OF LADY, ENSURING THAT ALL VOICES AND PERSPECTIVES ARE VALUED AND REPRESENTED IN OUR COMMUNITY.

INSPIRE JOY: ENCOURAGE A SENSE OF JOY AND FULFILLMENT IN THE CREATIVE PROCESS, MAKING ART A SOURCE OF HEALING AND CONNECTION.